STU1

Stanislaus Eric Stenbock (1860–1895), Count of Bogesund, was born in the South West England to Lucy Sophia Frerichs, an English cotton heiress, and Count Erich Stenbock, who was of a distinguished Swedish noble family of the Baltic German House of nobility in Reval. He inherited his family's estates in 1885 and returned to live in his manor house at Kolkbriefly for a period before returning to England. In his life he published three volumes of poetry and one collection of short stories, *Studies of Death*. He died as a result of alcoholism and opium addiction.

SNUGGLY BOOKS

STUDIES OF DEATH

ROMANTIC TALES, BY

ERIC, COUNT STENBOCK

THIS IS A SNUGGLY BOOK

Contents

STUDIES OF DEATH

Hylas

I WAS intending to paint a picture of David as the Shepherd, but nowhere could I find a suitable model for the face; there were several 'white and ruddy,' but none which had on them the impress of the born King, or the inspiration of the Psalmist. One day I was rowing up the river, and came across the very face I had been seeking for so long. He was a boy of about fifteen, clad in flannels, alone in a boat which he had moored to the shore of a little island in the middle of the river; he was occupied in sketching. 'This is lucky,' I thought, 'it will be a good excuse to begin a conversation,' so I rowed up to him, and saying that I was an artist, asked to see what he was drawing; he blushed, and showed me. Of course I had expected the usual smudged landscape; but imagine my surprise to find a certainly beautifully conceived drawing of Hylas by the river's brink, with the Nymph stretching out her arms towards him. He was merely copying the rushes and trees of the island as a background. The Hylas was not at all a bad portrait of himself, but my surprise was still greater to find that the face of the Nymph was an evident copy of my own last picture called 'The Siren,' which I had recently sold to a certain Professor Langton (at a very low price, as I knew the Professor was not well off and his genuine enthusiasm for my work was so refreshing after the inane compliments of those who thought it the 'thing' to admire me because I happened to be the 'fashion' just then). I praised the drawing, and pointed out one or two faults, then asked for paper and pencil, and reproduced the drawing as it should have been. The boy watched with ever-increasing eagerness; at last he said with a deep blush, 'May I ask you what your name is?'

'My name is Gabriel Glynde,' I replied.

'Ah, I thought so all the time you were drawing. Do you know, your pictures have always had a peculiar fascination for me; father has lots of them, at least *drawings*, only one *painting*, that one called "The Siren," from which I copied that: you must know father, he went to see your studio the other day;' then, blushing still deeper, 'May I come and see your studio too? '

'Certainly you may; but I ask something in return: that is, that you will sit as model for the "shepherd David." I guess from what you say that you are the son of Professor Langton; am I not right? May I ask what is your Christian name?'

'Oh, Lionel,' he said simply; 'there's only father and me; I don't mind being a model if you like, and will let me see your studio, though why you should think I should make a suitable David I am at a loss to understand.'

There was a mixture of simple boyishness, and at the same time education, about his way of talking which puzzled me, but the explanation was not difficult to unravel. We rowed down together: I took him to tea at an old wayside inn covered with honeysuckle, then went straight with him to his father's. He had told me all about himself on the way. He was his father's only son, he had never been to school, his father had taught him everything himself, he had no companions of his own age, and amused himself alone. He liked riding and rowing and swimming, but hated shooting and fishing (curious this, that he should share my own ingrained dislikes), but what he loved above all was drawing and painting; he had never learnt to draw, but he had always drawn ever since he could remember. His father knew everything, but could not draw, but was very fond of pictures, but nevertheless would not let him go to an art school, etc. So he prattled on. I could not help remarking that he seemed *very* much more educated than boys of his age usually are, though wholly unconscious of the fact, and yet, at the same time, showed a singular artlessness and innocence about the most common-place things.

Professor Langton received me with the utmost amiability, and the end of it was that I stayed there the evening. After he had sent his son to bed, he expounded to me his ideas on education. He did not approve of schools of any kind he said; boarding schools were an abomination, but day schools, perhaps, were a necessity. 'But in my case,' he said, 'happily *not*; indeed, what is the use of being a Professor if I cannot instruct my own boy?'

Well, the end of all this was, that having Lionel as a model, I took a great fancy to him, and the more I saw of him the less I liked the idea of his going to an Academy school. Perhaps to a boy ordinarily brought up the usual conversation of art students would not do much harm, but to Lionel—this exotic flower—I shuddered to think of it. I never before had had any pupils, wishing to be individual, and not to create a school, but then Lionel was of my school already. So the end of it was that I offered to take him as a gratuitous and exclusive pupil, for which his father was intensely grateful.

❋

Years passed by, and I taught him to draw and to paint very well; perhaps I impregnated him a little too much with my own individuality. I used to chuckle to myself, 'This is just like Leonardo da Vinci and Salaino. Critics in the future will be disputing which is a genuine "Glindio."' I do not mean by this that Lionel had no imagination or inventive power—on the contrary, he was, as I have said before, a 'genius,' an artist, born, not made—but merely that his style of execution was based on mine; indeed, I even hoped that he might surpass in my own line.

❋

One does not realise what a frightful responsibility one incurs in introducing one person to another. In nine cases out of ten nothing particular may ensue, but the tenth case may be the turning-point in a life for good or for evil. Thus it was when I introduced Lionel to Lady Julia Gore-Vere. When

I say introduced him, I did nothing of the kind; she was having tea with me in my studio, and Lionel, who I thought was going up the river that day (that was one of the reasons I had selected that day to ask her), suddenly walked in. Well! what could I do but introduce them.

Lady Julia bore the name Gore-Vere because she had two husbands, both alive and kicking, and through some anomaly of the Divorce Court, she could not legally ascertain whether she ought to bear the name of Mr. Gore or Mr. Vere, so she split the difference by giving herself both appellations. What her past was I did not know, and did not care to inquire—it was no concern of mine; what did concern me was that she bought my pictures. She was certainly the last person I should have liked Lionel to meet. She was a very lovely woman and very clever (when I say clever I do not merely mean sharp and witty, but really cultured), and when she talked about Art she really knew what she was talking about. Except for a moment of irritation, I did not see any particular harm. Lionel knew nothing about her; there was nothing remarkable in the fact that she took an interest in him; and he took a childish pleasure in showing her his sketches, which she criticised and admired, justly, for, as I have said before, they were remarkably good.

I had always thought of Lionel as a child, and never realised that he was now grown up. Happening to know Lady Julia's age, it did not occur to me that to people in general she looked a very great deal younger than she really was. Well, they met several times. One day Lionel said, 'How like Lady Julia is to your picture "The Siren."' I have always maintained that artists give models for faces, as much as faces give models for artists. I had done so many pictures since, I had quite forgotten about 'The Siren.' Now 'The Siren' was entirely an imaginative face, taken from no model at all, but when Lionel said so, it struck me she *was* like 'The Siren.' Then I thought of his drawing the first day I had met him. A disagreeable sensation and vague fear haunted me; I took to watch him more closely. Then the truth flashed upon me—he was hopelessly in love with her. She was doing her best to egg him on; what an idiot I was not to have seen that before, I who pretend to be observant of all things.

No, this would not do at all, it would be the ruin of his life. I must save him at any cost. Perhaps I had been wrong all the time, I had kept him too much under a glass case; perhaps if he had had more experience he would not have become so suddenly and completely infatuated. Oh, how wicked of her! I raged and gnashed my teeth. Had she not the whole world for prey that she could not spare this poor boy? What could he be to her? But then, perhaps, she did not realise what harm she was doing. I would go and expostulate with her myself; from what I knew of her she was by no means heartless.

So next day I called on her, and somewhat rudely came to the point at once. 'Why,' I said, 'do you seek to ruin that poor boy's life? You know whom I mean—Lionel. Surely such a conquest must be nothing to you?'

I spoke very bitterly, she answered calmly, 'You ask me why? I will tell you the reason quite simply: first, because I am jealous of him; secondly, because I thought you cared for me a little, and I thought I might make you jealous of me, and finally, because *I love you.*'

I was utterly dumfounded; for some time I could not speak at all. Then I said, 'If it is true, as you say, that you love me, do at least this one thing for me—spare *him.*' She answered in the same calm voice. 'There is one way to overcome the difficulty.' I went out without a word.

All that night I remained without sleep, thinking. 'There was one way to overcome the difficulty.' I had said I would save him at any cost, and the cost was to sacrifice myself. However unselfish one's motive may be, selfish considerations are inevitably intermingled. I thought, After all, the sacrifice is not so very terrible, the way out of the difficulty comparatively easy—I certainly liked her well enough, and now that my studio parties were on a much larger scale than heretofore, it would really be a great convenience to have a lady in the house. And then I thought, trying to be unselfish again, I shall be doing a good turn to her; by giving her my name I shall re-establish her reputation and people will soon forget that her name has ever been Gore or Vere. . . . Lionel would soon realise the absurdity of his own position, and of course would not think of making love to my wife.

So next morning I wrote to Lady Julia, asking her if she would be willing to exchange the ambiguous name of Gore-Vere for that of Glynde. She wrote back to say she would be very pleased to accept my offer, but she thought I might have phrased it more kindly.

Fortunately Lionel was going away the next day on a walking tour by himself (a thing which he was very fond of doing), for I could not bring myself to tell Lionel about it just yet, or indeed till the whole thing was over. There was no reason whatever for delay, so we arranged to be married quietly in Paris before a Maire, as, for obvious reasons, it would be better not to be married in London. When the marriage was over I made up my mind to write to Lionel. I tore up several letters in various styles; at last I resolved to adopt the flippantly facetious. I said, 'I am now in Paris, and *who* do you think is my companion? You will never guess—Lady Julia Gore-Vere, only her name isn't Gore-Vere now, but Glynde, because I have married her; but it won't make any difference, you must call her Lady Julia all the same.'

To this letter there was no response; to this I attached but little importance. 'Of course,' I thought, 'he will be a little sulky at first, but he will soon get over it; his innate sense of humour will show him how foolish he has been.'

In spite of all people might say against my wife, there could be no more charming travelling companion, always amusing and amused, and intelligently critical; indeed, if I had not always had the haunting thought of Lionel, I think we should have enjoyed ourselves very much.

Will you understand me if I say that I was sorry to find out my wife's past was by no means as black as it was painted; indeed, she was much more the wronged than the wrongdoer. This, I suppose, is inverted selfishness; it is a luxury to pose as a hero. What was my heroic self-sacrifice? Simply getting a charming wife, who really loved me, and who had never loved any one else before. I wrote to Lionel once more—a long, lively letter describing the places we had been to, interspersed with graphic sketches of persons and places. To this again I received no answer. But then as I had addressed it to the last country place where I knew Lionel had been staying, I came to the conclusion he could not have received it, possibly having left no address behind him.

At last we came home; I learned that Lionel was staying with his father. I sent a note, saying: 'I insist on seeing you. Come this evening. Waiting for an answer.'

There was *no* answer; but in the evening Lionel came in person.

Lionel, I say? Could *this* be Lionel? He was utterly changed. All youth and buoyancy had gone from him; he rather dragged himself along than walked; he was quite pale, and wore a look of utter, absolute dejection. I tried to pretend to take no notice.

'Well, Lionel,' I said, with sham cheerfulness, 'what have *you* been doing all this time?' He answered in a dull, apathetic voice, 'painting a picture.'

'A picture? What about?'

'You will get it the day after to-morrow,' he said in the same dull monotone.

'Child, what has come over you? Why do you keep aloof from me? Why do you not answer my letters?'

'I think it is somewhat needless for you to ask that question,' he said.

'No, but tell me—explain,' I cried, stretching out my hands to him. He went backwards to the other end of the room, and then said in a voice filled with tears, 'You have taken from me all that I loved; I should not have thought that of *you*. Of course you had a perfect right to do so, but still, at least, you might have told me first.'

'*All* that you loved?' I said.

'Yes! *All* except yourself, and you have killed my love for you,' he said, almost with a wail.

'But, Lionel, listen; I do not love her.'

'Do you consider that an excuse?' he said fiercely; 'if you *did* I might forgive you; but as it is I cannot.'

'But listen, child,' I cried; 'hear me out; it is not *her* that I love but *you*; it was to save you from what I thought would be your utter ruin that I married her.'

'A strange way of showing love to break my heart,' he said in the same spiritless voice as before; 'Good-bye,' and then he turned his back on me, and held out his left hand—it was quite cold, and fell limp to his side; he turned once round as he opened the door with a look of mute reproach which will haunt me for ever.

The day after tomorrow I took up the morning paper, and saw this:—

SHOCKING ACCIDENT WHILE BATHING.

'Near —— Island (the island where I first met Lionel), the body of a young man was found yesterday. There was little difficulty in identifying the body as that of Mr. Lionel Langton, a young artist of much promise, as his clothes were on the shore, and a pocket-book containing cards and letters was found in the coat pocket, and also as Mr. Langton was well-known in this neighbourhood, being particularly fond of bathing at this spot. The fact of his being drowned has caused much astonishment, as he was known to be a remarkably good swimmer. Death was attributed to sudden cramp. His father, Professor Langton, was immediately telegraphed for, and seemed quite overcome with grief. He deposed that lately he had been much distressed about his son; he had been unwell and very depressed, also strange in his manner, for which he, his father, could assign no cause.'

Hardly had I read this, when there was a violent knock at the door, and two men came in bringing a picture. Never had I seen anything so good from Lionel's hand; it was simply wonderful. It represented Hylas lying at the bottom of a river, seen through water. The figure of Hylas was a portrait of himself as he was when I first saw him, but somehow into the closed eyes he had infused the expression which I had last seen in his face. Looking down, reflected in the water, was my own face. Starting up, I caught a sight of my face in a mirror; by what prescience did he know that I should look thus on hearing the tidings of his death?

Narcissus

MY father died before I was born, and my mother in giving birth to me, so I was born at once to a title and a fortune. I merely mention this to show that Fortune, in a way seemed from the first to smile upon me. The one passion of my life was beauty, and I thought myself specially *fortunate* that I realised my own ideal in myself. Even now that I am writing I look round the room, and see portraits of myself at various stages of my life: as a child, a boy, and a young man. Never have I seen a face as lovely as my own was. That glorious classic outline, those large, lustrous, dark blue eyes, that curled gold hair, like woven sunshine, that divinely curved mouth and exquisite grace of lips, that splendid poise of neck and throat! I was not vain in the proper sense of the word, for vanity means desire for the approbation of others, and getting up oneself to please others. But I, on the contrary, did not care what others thought; I would remain for hours before the mirror in a kind of ecstasy. No! no single picture I had ever seen could come up to me!

I was spoilt as a child. At school my life was made easy for me. Others did my impositions, and masters overlooked my peccadilloes; and if the boys of my own form hated and envied me, they knew that if they dared lift a finger against me, they would have their lives thrashed out of them by my champions in the upper forms. I do not mean to say by this that my school career was not a success in the ordinary sense of the word; because, besides being beautiful, I was brilliantly clever, and learnt in a day what it would take others months to learn. And if I say I was spoilt, I at least was not pettish and fretful as spoilt children usually are; on the contrary, I was invariably amiable, perhaps because my will was never gainsaid. Unlike most in whom the aesthetic sense is abnormally developed, I had absolutely no passions. I did not love anyone—but then, I allowed myself very gracefully to be loved, and always sought to please those who loved me, so that I actually got the reputation of being unselfish.

This was all very well as a boy. When I became of age I was launched into society. Women, one and all, appeared to fall in love with me. I don't mean fortune-seekers and tuft-hunters, but such as had the same wealth and social position as myself. I was congratulated on my conquests, and told that my admirers were celebrated beauties. Beauties, indeed! What was their beauty to mine? I did not understand women or their sentiments at all; but I had read several novels, and tried to be amiable to one and all, and make love to them in the conventional way, as I had read. One time there appeared on the scene a girl who was considered dazzlingly beautiful. She really was rather handsome. She was the daughter of a Mexican millionaire, and, of course, was sought after by everyone. Indeed, I was reminded at the time of the Bab Ballad, 'Dukes with the humble maiden dealt,' and, unlike Duke Baily and Duke Humphey, they were willing to cast their coronets and their lands at her feet. But she, unlike the heroine of the Bab Ballad, preferred my 'miserable and grovelling' self. I must say here that my *vanity* was this time rather flattered; it rather pleased me to think that they should be put in the background for my sake, and I was as amiable to her as possible, and used to take her out everywhere.

She was certainly clever, but there was a certain savage passionateness about her nature that jarred upon me.

One day her father said to me, 'You can't think how glad I am to hear that you are engaged to my daughter. As we happen to be alone together, perhaps you wouldn't mind if we settle all the particulars of this business. I intend to behave very handsomely to her, and will give her a dowry of———.' (Good heavens! This parvenu!)

'Engaged to your daughter!' I cried, 'there has been no such understanding between us. I am extremely sorry, but I cannot imagine who could have been your informant. The information is wholly and entirely false.'

'What?' he said, 'not engaged to Enriqueta? What on earth do you mean? Do you suppose I should have allowed you to go about with my girl as you have been doing? Again, I ask, what do you mean?'

'I am sorry,' I replied, 'that you should have been labouring under such a misapprehension. In proof that I mean what I say, I will avoid all intercourse with your daughter for the future. And I can scarcely believe she is under the same misapprehension as yourself.' With that remark I left the house abruptly.

A short time afterwards, when I was seated by the fire in my drawing-room reading, who should walk in suddenly but Enriqueta herself, with furiously flashing eyes. She looked like a fiend incarnate. The emblem of anger in the abstract. I remember at that moment the words of the proverb flashing across me, 'Non est ira sicut ira mulieris.'

'So,' she said, 'this is how you behave! Well, then, take that!' and saying this, she threw a fluid from a glass phial into my face. It was not vitriol; that would have blinded me: this, unfortunately, did not!

A sudden smart on one side of the face, then gradually the whole face corroded. The cheeks fell in, the flesh part of the nose dropped off, the hair came out in handfuls, several of the teeth dropped out, the mouth contorted into a ghastly grin, the eyes became cavernous and horrible, denuded of eyebrows and lashes. I saw myself in a mirror *once*; anything more loathsome it would be impossible to imagine.

Some friends called to sympathise with me, but on no consideration would I admit any one. I had every mirror in the house broken and thrown away, and could scarcely bear to look into a washing-basin. I spoke to my servants from behind a screen, and lived utterly alone, and by night. I had only one opportunity of air and exercise, so I managed to bribe the policeman to let me into Hyde Park just before the gates closed at night, and there I would wander about all night through, till at dawn the gates opened again, when I would hurry home.

One night, when I was going on my usual lonely walk, the wailing voice of a child came out of the darkness.

'Do please help me,' it cried, 'mother left me here, and said she would come back directly, and now I have heard the clock strike the hour four times, and mother hasn't come back, and I am blind, quite blind.'

I lit my lantern; it was a child of about nine or ten years old. It was clad in rags—yet the voice had the accent of a gentleman.

I said, 'It's impossible to get out now; you must wait till the gates open in the morning. Come and sit here? Are you hungry?'

'Yes,' said the child simply.

'Well, then, let's have something to eat.' Then I undid my knapsack, wherein I always took with me provisions of various dainties, and wine, for my nocturnal meal, and spreading a napkin, prepared a repast.

Then the child told me his story. I cannot repeat it in the artless way he told it; I can only give the gist of it. He was very delicate-looking, with a very sweet face, and an infinite pathos in the expression of the closed eyes. It appeared he lived alone with his mother. His name, he said, was Tobit: that he had been born blind, and did not know what seeing anything meant. He did not think he had any surname; his mother was always called 'Bonny Bess,' because people said she was so *handsome.*

'What does handsome mean?' he asked. I shuddered.

'Oh!' I said, 'it means good-looking; but it's no use being handsome. It's better to be good.'

He said his mother was very unkind to him, and was always beating him; but there was a gentleman, who used to come about every three months, who was very kind to him, and used to bring him presents, and give his mother money. The gentleman was an officer, he said. He always knew when the gentleman was coming, because his mother did not beat him for three weeks beforehand, because one time the gentleman had seen some bruises on him, and had been very angry, and had beaten his mother. And when the gentleman had gone, his mother had said: 'If you dare to tell the gentleman anything about me again, I'll thrash you within an inch of your life.'

The gentleman used to talk to him, and take him out for walks. But all toys the gentleman brought him his mother would take away from him, and sell them in order to get drink. Twice he had taken him to a place called 'the country' for a whole week. There were flowers and birds singing; then he was really happy.

'The only thing she didn't take away from me,' he said, 'is this: and from his pocket he produced a penny whistle, 'because she said she could not get anything for it, and I might go and play it in the street. Then, perhaps, people would give me pennies.' Then he proceeded to perform on the penny whistle. Good heavens! I had no idea that out of a thing like that so much tone could be elicited! He began with a well-known organ-grinder tune, then came variations filled with roulades. I was simply astounded. 'A great many people give me pennies: he said, naïvely, 'but mother takes them all away from me.'

One day he had overheard the gentleman quarrelling with his mother. 'Then why don't you make me an honest woman?' she had said.

'It would be quite impossible to make *you* an honest woman. Shut up your cant. You know perfectly well I can't marry you. Even if I could, I wouldn't. I only wish to God I could take poor little Tobit away with me.'

'Rob a mother of her only child,' said the mother, whimpering, 'fortunately the law of England does not allow that.'

'Blast your infernal humbug!' said the gentleman, 'I know you don't care a hang about the child. You only want the money. I feel quite certain that you ill-treat him, though he has never said a word about it. Bah! You talk of being an *honest* woman. Look how the child is dressed—look how you are!'

As soon as the gentleman had gone his mother seized upon him, and beat him so severely that he screamed for help. A man came in, and seized her arms and pinned her to the ground.

'Look here,' the man had said, 'that's enough of that, you she-devil! If you try that sort of game again you'll get the worst of it!'

The last time he saw the gentleman he had been more tender than ever before. He had felt hot tears falling on his face.

'Poor little Tobit!' he had said. 'I am going away to a far country, and perhaps may never see you again.'

Then he had heard the gentleman talking to his mother. 'Look here, Bess,' he said, 'this is all the money I can scrape together, and this must last you out while I am away. But I hope to be back soon, and then I shall have higher pay.'

He had cried for many days afterwards, which made his mother very angry. One day, after waiting some time, he had asked when the gentleman would be coming back again from the far country. 'He won't be coming back again at all,' answered his mother snappishly. 'He's dead—got shot in Africa, blast him! Get out and play the whistle.'

He had gone out in the streets, and cried very much at first, and then it seems he put his grief into music: 'Because,' he said, 'he had got more pennies than he had ever got before.' A little while after he had heard his mother whispering to a man. 'Damn it!' said the man, 'we can't take that bloody brat with us.'

'Oh, I'll manage that,' the mother had said. And that evening his mother had taken him out in to the park, and had told him she wanted to speak with somebody, and was coming back directly, and told him to stay there. He had heard a man's voice, but his mother had never come back again.

Fortunately, as soon as the child had finished his story he went fast asleep. I do not know what I

should have said. Its utter loathsomeness reminded me of the one sight I had had of my own face.
At dawn I woke the child up. Putting down my
thick black veil I turned home, taking the child
with me. I sent a servant to make inquiries, and
the result was as I had expected—the mother had
decamped with all her possessions, and not paid
the rent.

So at last one consolation was sent me. After
having been so long alone, at last I had a companion—one who would not recoil from the sight of
me. I determined to give up my nocturnal life,
and managed to secure a cottage in a remote and
desolate part of the country, where one could walk
for miles without seeing any one, and in mercy to
my servants, stationed them in the nearest town,
requiring them only to bring me provisions and
do the house once a day.

The child was delighted with the country. His
placid, absolute happiness, in all his blindness,
was much more than I had ever experienced in
the delight in beauty by the sense of sight. He
was very intelligent and phenomenally good, and
I managed to teach him music, in which he took
the keenest pleasure. The piano, of course, was a
thing unknown to him before. His only instrument had been a penny whistle!

One day I read in the paper that an operation had been successfully performed by a certain eminent oculist on a person born blind. An awful struggle rose in my mind; supposing the child could be made to see! I thought of the frightful blank all things which to me had seemed of the greatest value must be to him, and was I to deprive him of that? Then, if he could see, and saw me, he would recoil from me in horror. But then I knew that my health was failing—that I should not live long, and was I, just to gratify my own selfishness for a short time, to condemn him to perpetual darkness, when it lay within my reach to save him? It was, as I said before, a frightful struggle. At last I decided I would consult the oculist. I took the child to London.

The oculist came, and said in his case the operation would be quite simple—not nearly so difficult as the case mentioned in the papers. It would merely require—well, I don't know what. I know nothing of medical terms, so I consented to have the operation performed. The child was given chloroform, and, the operation completed, his eyes were bound with bandages, which I was told to take off on the third day.

On the third day I did so. I had always thought that the blind, even though born blind, made visual images of things. In his case it was not so. The operation had been successful, and he could see. He knew well enough, by the touch, what a chair or a table was, but I had the greatest difficulty in explaining this or that was a chair or table as he saw it. He seemed quite dazed. Then he said ultimately:—

'And you are the most beautiful person in the world!'

The Death of a Vocation

IT would not seem surprising at first sight that Seraphine de Sainte Amaranthe, incontestably the most beautiful girl of the Paris season, and one of the richest of heiresses, should have been married to the Marquis Celestin de Laval, the last representative of one of the most ancient families in France, and that being married 'they lived happily ever afterwards.' The incident appears entirely commonplace, and rather more fit for the *Morning Post* than anywhere else. But to those who were more intimate with either party, it was an occasion of great surprise.

The title of De Sainte Amaranthe was not of very ancient date. Indeed, ill-natured persons assert his name was originally Joseph Levi; and there certainly was a Hebraic strain about him. But then had he not vast wealth? and was he not married to a 'mondaine' of the first water? And Seraphine herself had received the usual education of the Parisian mondaine. At the time I am speaking of (I wish to narrate the actual facts of this case), she was being dragged about to balls and parties, after having first of all been spoilt as a child, and then shut up in a convent.

She was certainly a very beautiful girl, with dark hair, and liquid, spiritual eyes. But somehow she did not take to balls and parties, but hankered after her convent, where she determined to become a nun, of which of course her parents would not hear. She was not morose, and did not mind going to the theatre, and things of that kind. But then she would say, 'Yes, this is all great fun, but it is not my life.' The one thing she loathed and detested was a ball. She had one of those graceful figures which would look well even if clothed in a sack; and she was far from being awanting in the feminine love of dress, and managed to clothe herself very well. She was also a graceful dancer. But the inane compliments and conversation, and the lasciviously amorous looks of her many admirers, filled her with unutterable loathing. The celebrated 'sport' and' ''ighlif' man, the Duc de Morlaix, whom her parents desired to thrust upon her, was her special abhorrence. Then how pleased were her parents when she seemed to be taking a fancy to the Marquis de Laval!

Celestin de Laval in many respects resembled her, though of course he had seen much more of the world. He was a dilettante in literature, art, and music; and somewhat luxurious in his tastes. He had determined for some years to become a monk; always the courage failed him to take the final step. He would say: 'All these things I can get on without; they are not necessary to me. I can easily give them up.' His friends would say, 'Oh yes! we believe that.' But anyhow, although in touch with every latest form of modern thought, he did not lose his religion. Indeed it was in connection with that he first met Mademoiselle de Ste. Amaranthe. He was a good-looking man, with an intellectual type of face, of about thirty. It happened one day when he was in a church at Salut; he happened to be seated next a lady, who dropped her prayer-book, which he handed to her. He was rather struck with her beauty, as he was with all beautiful things, though none of his friends ever remembered his having loved a woman.

In France, almost the Oriental system of the Harem is kept up. A man may be even intimately acquainted with another man in restaurants and cafés, and such like places, and yet never have been introduced into his family; and Celestin had frequently met here and there the Baron de Ste. Amaranthe. One day, meeting him at some *cercle,* Ste. Amaranthe begged him to honour him with his presence at a large ball that he was giving in celebration of his daughter's birthday. Now, if there was one thing that Celestin hated more than another, it was a ball. Not having an excuse handy, he was obliged to accept. So he went. Great was his surprise to find there the girl whom he had met a few days before in church. He was obliged out of common politeness to engage her for one dance. She said to him, with a singularly candid expression—

'I'm sure you don't like dancing any more than I do.'

He answered, 'No, I do not. Let us rather go and sit out there in the cool, if you do not mind. I think we have seen one another before.'

'Oh yes,' she answered; 'it was at the Madeleine; you picked up my prayer-book. You at least go to church. Oh, I am so utterly tired of this eternal round of balls and parties. Cannot they leave me in peace? I wonder that you should like this sort of thing.'

'But,' answered the Marquis, 'I don't like this sort of thing at all. I was obliged to accept this invitation'; then blushing and stammering, 'Of course, mademoiselle, I did not mean——' Just at this moment the Duc de Morlaix came to claim his partner, and so saved him from the difficulty 'of things one would rather have left unsaid.'

The long and short of it was that the Marquis de Laval soon became an intimate of the house. The Baron was constantly inviting him to dinner, and the Baron took every opportunity of leaving them alone together, under the impression that he had taken a fancy to her, and she to him, and that she might thus make a brilliant match.

In a way, certainly they had taken a fancy to one another. They had many tastes in common: it was a relief to her, after the many smirking admirers, to find a man who treated her as an intellectual sympathetic being. And he had perhaps very much the same feeling with regard to her. After a time they became confidential. One day she said to him, 'You know my resolution is the same as yours. You have freedom and I have not. I intend to enter a religious order, and what am I to do? Certainly my parents keep me as closely confined as I should be in the most enclosed order, and they go on insisting on my being married to one of these wretched creatures with stick-up collars, and an inane face, whom I loathe the sight of. You know you are the only man who has ever been at least a friend to me: and my mother does not like me to have girl friends, and indeed if I had any I do not think I should like them. *Their ideal* of life appears to be that which is *my* repulsion. So what am I to do? It is really to you only, who might understand me, that I can appeal for advice.'

'Well,' he answered slowly, 'there is only one possible escape from the difficulty. You will be somewhat surprised to hear what I propose. But if you think about it, you will find it is not so startling after all. Namely, that you and I should go through a nominal form of marriage, and live together as brother and sister for a little while; then you would be free to do as you liked. And we would then part and go to our separate convents.'

She trembled a little, and said, 'But supposing you should come to love some other woman, and I were to go into a convent, I should be an everlasting drag upon you.'

He answered, 'I thought you knew me well enough to suppose that. Besides, I think, according to the laws of our Church, if I may speak plainly, a marriage without consummation is considered null and void. But there's no need to trouble about that. You seem to doubt my vocation.'

She took his hand, and said, 'I was only afraid for *your* sake; if you really mean what you say—well, 'tis the will of God.'

The delight of the Baron, on hearing his daughter was engaged, was immense: and when the Marquis de Laval came to him to make arrangements, he was amiably prepared to behave very generously towards his only child. Great was his surprise when De Laval refused to accept any dowry whatsoever. After a great deal of pressing he said—

'Well, if you insist upon it, you can provide her with her trousseau. And though both of us would rather be married as privately as possible, if you wish to have a train of bridesmaids and a High Mass with full orchestra, you are at liberty to pay for it. But after she is my wife I will not touch a penny of her money. I have, *Dieu merci!* quite enough to support us both.'

So they were married in grand state, and this was of course reported as fashionable intelligence in all the papers. They first of all went to his chateau near Nantes in Brittany, where Laval's mother was rather astonished at their occupying separate rooms. Indeed, the only occasion he entered his wife's room was when they said the breviary together, in preparation for their monastic life. Then they went travelling about Italy. In a quiet way they amused themselves very much, and found they had still more points in common than they had thought before. And making no acquaintances, they found themselves mutually a necessity to one another. They became literally brother and sister, except, as is unprecedented in brothers and sisters, they never quarrelled once.

One day, a year after their marriage, they came back to his house in Paris. They decided to take the final step. He suggested, half in jest, half in earnest, that she should put on the habit of the Franciscan tertiaries, to see what she would look like as a nun; which she did. He looked at her, tears gathering in his eyes.

'O Seraphine!' he said, 'I shall miss you very much.'

Suddenly she threw her arms round him and kissed him, for the first time, passionately.

'No, dear,' she cried; 'I cannot leave you. I cannot live without you!'

Just then there was a loud knock and ring at the door. She went down to the door in her nun's dress. A wretched girl was running along the street; then she stumbled over something on the doorstep. It cried piteously; she took it up: it was a child of about one year old, wrapt up in squalid rags: it put out its arms towards her: when she took it in her arms it ceased to cry. She took it up, and without a word laid it upon her husband's lap. The child stretched out its soft clinging arms towards Celestin, and turned his forget-me-not-like eyes upon him; it remained quite quiet. She went out of the room noiselessly. After a time she came back, arrayed in her bridal dress. She sat down beside him, and put the child between them. Then they sat there for a long time, hand in hand, in utter silence.

Viol D'amor

ONE TIME there was much in vogue a peculiarly sweet-toned kind of violin, or rather, to be accurate, something between a viola and a violoncello. Now they are no longer made. This is the history of the last one that was ever made, I think. This somewhat singular story might in some way explain why they are made no longer. But though I am a poetess, and consequently inclined to believe in the unlikely, this I do not suppose was the history of Viol d'Amors in general. I may add, by way of prefix, that its peculiar sweetness of tone was produced by the duplicated reverberation of strings below, with yet another reverberation within the sounding-board. But to my story.

I was once in Freiburg—Freiburg in Baden, I mean. I went one Sunday to High Mass at the

Cathedral. Beethoven's glorious Mass in C was magnificently rendered by a string quartet. I was specially impressed by the first violin, a dignified, middle-aged man, with a singularly handsome face, reminding one of the portraits of Leonardo da Vinci. He was dressed in a mediaeval-looking black robe; and he played with an inspiration such as I have seldom, if ever, heard. There was likewise a most beautiful boy's treble. Boys' voices, lovely in their 'timbre' as nothing else, are generally somewhat wanting in their expression. This one united the most exquisite 'timbre' with the most complete possible expression. I was going to stay in Freiburg some time, as I knew people there. The first violinist had aroused my curiosity. I learnt that he was an Italian, a Florentine, of the ancient noble family of da Ripoli. But he was now a maker of musical instruments, not very well off—who nevertheless played at the Cathedral for love, not money; also that the beautiful treble was his youngest son, and he was a widower with five children. As he interested me, I sought to procure an introduction, which I succeeded in getting without difficulty.

He lived in one of those beautiful old houses which linger still in towns like Freiburg. He seemed somewhat surprised that an Englishwoman should go out of her way to visit him. Fortunately I was familiar with Italian, being myself an Italian on the mother's side, and was at that time on my way to Italy. He received me with much affability. I was ushered into a long Gothic room, done in black oak: there was a very beautiful Gothic window, which was open. It was spring-time, and the most delightful weather. There was a strong scent of May about the room, emanating from a hawthorn-tree immediately opposite the window, which had the extraordinary peculiarity of bearing red and white blossoms at the same time. The room was full of all sorts of odds and ends of things—caskets, vessels, embroideries—all exquisitely artistic. He told me these were executed by a son and daughter of his. We began to interest one another, and had a long talk. As we were talking, in walked a tall, grave-looking young man. He was of the pure Etruscan type—dark, and indeed somewhat sombre.

With a perturbed air, not noticing me, he suddenly made this singular remark, 'Saturn is in conjunction with the moon: I fear that ill may betide Guido.'

'This is my son Andrea,' his father explained, 'my eldest son; he goes in much for astronomy, and indeed also for astrology, in which you probably do not believe.'

At that moment in walked another young man. This was the second son, Giovanni. He was also dark, like his brother, and tall, but had a very pleasing smile. He reminded me rather of the portrait of Andrea del Sarto. It was he who manufactured—to use the word in its proper sense—these beautiful objects which were lying about the table. After him came in two sisters: the elder, whose name was Anastasia, was a tall, stately girl, with dark hair and grey eyes, but pale face: very much like the type we are familiar with from the pictures of Dante Gabriel Rossetti. The younger sister was quite different: she was fair, but fair in the Italian manner: that glorious, ivory-white complexion so different from the pink and white of the North. Her hair was of that glorious red-gold colour which we see in Titian's pictures, but her eyes were dark. Her name was Liperata. It appears Anastasia was the eldest of the family, then came Andrea and Giovanni, then Liperata, and lastly, Guido, whom I had not seen as yet.

I omitted to mention, though it does not seem here of any significance at all, that Anastasia wore a blue gown of somewhat stiff mediaeval cut, but very graceful all the same. I learnt afterwards it was both designed and made by herself.

Presently there entered the room a boy of about fourteen. This was Guido. He was fairer than his brothers, though also somewhat of the Etruscan type, and was not so tall for his age. He looked singularly fragile and delicate. His complexion was more delicate than a rose-petal: he had those long, supple, sensitive hands which indicate the born musician. His somewhat long hair, of a shade of brown, had a shadow of gold on it, as if it had been golden once. But in his strange-coloured eyes, which were grey-blue, streaked with yellow bars, there was a far-off look, like a light not of this world, shining on a slowly-rippling river of music. He went straight to the window, also not noticing there was a stranger in the room, and said, 'Ah, how beautiful the May-tree is! I shall only see it bloom once more.' He seemed indeed to be looking through the blooming hawthorn at that pale planet Saturn, which then was, for *it*, singularly large and brilliant. Andrea shuddered, but Giovanni bent down and kissed him, and said, 'What, Guido, another fit of melancholia?'

As you may imagine, I was interested in this singular family, and soon our acquaintance ripened into intimacy. It was to Anastasia that I was specially drawn, and she to me. Anastasia inherited the musical tastes of her father, and was herself no mean executant on the violin.

Andrea was not only occupied with astronomy and astrology, but even with alchemy and such like things, and occult sciences generally.

The whole family was very superstitious. They seemed to take astrology and magic as matters of course. But Andrea was by far the most superstitious of them all. It was Giovanni who was the breadwinner of the family, together with his special sister, Liperata, who assisted him in his work, and herself did the most charming embroideries. The only thing was that their materials were too costly, and required a large outlay to be made before they could sell anything.

For though the musical instruments the father produced were super-excellent of their kind, and fetched large prices, he took so much care about his work that he was sometimes years in producing one violin. He was then absorbed in one idea, in producing a Viol d'Amor, an instrument which he said was the most beautiful in all the world, and which had unjustly fallen into disuse. And *his* Viol d'Amor was to excel all others that had ever been made. He had left Florence, he said, because he could not stand this great Republic (for though of one of the most ancient noble families, he was an ardent Republican) being converted into the capital of a tenth-rate monarchy. 'They will be taking Rome next,' he said. And he did not know that what he was saying was soon to come true.

They were not well off, certainly, but it was Anastasia who managed the household and cared for every one. And she was the most excellent of manageresses. And so their life was very simple, but nevertheless was elegant and refined.

I very often enjoyed their simple, truly Italian hospitality, recompensing them by purchasing some specimens of Giovanni's excellent workmanship, and a violin from the old Signor da Ripoli, which I have still, and would not part with for the world. Though, alas! I myself cannot play upon it. To cut a long story short, I had to go on with my journey, but I did not wholly lose sight of them, so to speak, and I corresponded frequently with Anastasia.

––––––––––––

One day, just about a year afterwards, I received the following letter from Anastasia:—

'DEAR CECILIA,—A great calamity has fallen upon us. It is so out of the common that you would hardly believe it. Of course you know how my father is devoted to his Viol d'Amor. You also know that we are all rather superstitious, but none to the same degree as Andrea. It appears that one day Andrea was poring into some old book, which was in that mongrel tongue, half Latin and half Italian, before the days of Dante, when he came across a passage (you know, I know nothing about the manufacture of musical instruments; but it appears that leather thongs are necessary to procure the complete vibration of the Viol d'Amor). In this passage it said that preternatural sweetness of tone could be procured if the thongs were made of the skin of those who loved the maker most. —[I had heard of this superstition before: I think there is some story in connection with Paganini of a similar nature, but nevertheless quite different. For as the legend goes about Paganini, the strings of a violin were made of the entrails of a person, which necessitated their murder; but here it would appear from the rest of the letter it did not do so, and was a freewill offering.]—Andrea conceived the fantastic idea of cutting off part of his own skin and having it tanned unbeknown to our father, telling him he had got it from the Clinic, because he had heard human leather was the best. To effect this he had to invoke the assistance of Giovanni, who, as you know, is so skilful with all instruments, and is also, as perhaps you do *not* know, a most skilful surgeon.

'Giovanni, not to be outdone by his brother, performed the same operation on himself. They were obliged to confide in me, and, as you know, I am very good as a nurse, and clever at bandages and such like. So I managed, with a little bandaging, and nursing, and sewing up the scars, to get them quite well again in a very short time. Of course no word of this was ever said to Liperata or Guido. And now comes the dreadful part of my story. How Guido could have divined anything I cannot understand. The only explanation I can offer is this. He is a very studious boy, and very fond of poring into the old books in Andrea's library. He might have seen the same passage, and with his extraordinary quick intuition have guessed. Anyhow he appears to have gone to some quack Jew doctor, and had a portion of his skin cut off in the same manner, and brought the skin to his brothers to be dealt with in the same way, which it *was*. The operation had been performed badly, and, as you know, the child is very delicate, and it has had the most disastrous results. He is hopelessly ill, and we do not know what to do. Of course we cannot tell our father. It is equally impossible to tell a doctor. Fortunately our father does not believe in doctors and trusts in *us*. It is a good thing all three of us know something of medical science: I think things are getting a little better. He rallied a little yesterday, and asked to be taken from his bed to the sofa in the long room. At his own request he was placed just opposite the May-tree, with the window open. This seemed to revive him. He became, comparatively speaking, quite animated, especially when a slight wind blew some of the red and white blossoms on to his coverlet. Giovanni and I have some hope, but Andrea has not. Liperata of course does not understand what it all means. Nor does our father, who is intensely anxious about Guido, whom he loves best of us all. —Ever affectionately,

'ANASTASIA.'

'P.S. —Good news at last! the Viol d'Amor is completed. Father came down and played it to us. Oh! what a divine tone it has! Guido first burst into tears, and then seemed to grow quite well again for some time afterwards. Father left the Viol d'Amor with me, that I should play to Guido whenever he wished it. Yes, there *is* hope after all, whatever Andrea may say.'

————————

Not long afterwards I received another letter from Anastasia in deep mourning. It ran thus:—

'The worst has happened. Last Friday, after having been for several days considerably better, Guido seemed almost himself again. I was alone with him in the long room. (One thinks of trivialities in great grief; I was wearing that same blue dress I had on when I first saw you.) There was a wind, also rain, which pattered against the window-pane, and the wind blew the blossoms of the May-tree like red-white snow to the ground. This seemed to depress Guido. He begged me to sing to him, and accompany myself on the Viol d'Amor. "It is so sweet of tone," he said, with a sweet, sad smile. "I am rather tired, though I do not feel much pain now. I shall not see the hawthorn bloom again."

'I began to sing an old Etruscan ballad—one of those songs that linger about the country parts of Tuscany, of a very simple, plaintive cadence, accompanied softly on the Viol d'Amor. It would be soothing, I thought, at any rate. And it was. Guido laid his head back and closed his eyes. Gradually the rain ceased and the wind stilled. Guido looked up. "That is better," he said, "I was afraid of the wind and the rain; and *you* stopped them with the Viol d'Amor! Look! the moon is beginning to shine again." It was a full moon, and it shone through the hawthorn-tree, making strange shadows on the window, and one ray shot direct on Guido's pale face. "Go on singing," he said faintly. So I sang on, and played on the Viol d'Amor. I felt some dreadful presentiment. I dared not stop singing and playing. It seemed that a shadow literally crept through the doorway, and came up to the bed, and bent over it. Then suddenly all the strings of the Viol d'Amor snapped! A strange wail seemed to come out of the sounding-board. I dropped it, and looked! Then I saw it was too late.

'Father took the Viol d'Amor and broke it in pieces, and cast it into the fire. His silent agony is too terrible to describe. I cannot tell you any more now.'

I was in Freiburg once again, and of course the first thing I did was to go and see my old friends. The Signor da Ripoli was very much aged. He still plays in the Cathedral. Did he, or did he not, ever know what had happened? Anyhow, he has made no further attempt to construct a Viol d'Amor; nor may the word even be mentioned in his presence.

Giovanni and Liperata have gone back to Italy, where they have set up a workshop for themselves. It is rumoured that Liperata is shortly to be married. But Anastasia remains with her father. I do not think that she will ever marry. Andrea has become a victim to settled melancholy. He lives quite by himself in a lonely tower. It was he who had the following inscription put on Guido's tomb:—

'La musica e l'Amor che move
il Sole e l'altre Stelle.'

The Egg of the Albatross

THE TOP of a disused lighthouse, surrounded by the sea, hardly seems to be a convenient or desirable residence for a little girl. This was the residence of Marina.

The people of Varenha did not seem to think there was anything very extraordinary about it. She had always been there: and when her father and mother died, they left her there all alone. Besides, there was something uncanny about her; and although she was a familiar figure in the town, and in fact rather a pet, at the same time people thought it just as well that she should live a little way off.

Varenha is an island in the West Indies not much known to the general public; but, nevertheless, many foreigners alight there in search of rare orchids and butterflies, and particularly of the eggs of waterfowl, who have there one of their greatest fastnesses. Such foreigners as do come thither are mostly wealthy people, and have yachts of their own, and on them the island thrives. It is only every now and then that a steamer touches there.

When I say Marina's father and mother died in the lighthouse I am not strictly accurate, because they were not her father and mother: and she, instead of being found under the traditional gooseberry bush, was hauled up in a mackerel net at the early age of three. Where she came from, and what she was, nobody ever knew. When she was picked up she could not speak at all. She was not drowned: on the contrary, she was swimming about quite naturally, as a puppy or kitten might do. According to the best authorities, she had the peculiar fairness and other characteristics of the Octoroon. But people generally regarded her as something not of this world. She did not seem to understand or respond to any known language; but she soon learnt to talk Portuguese. The old people, whose only child had been drowned years ago, became devoted to this strange sea-baby, whom they called Marina, from her origin.

A new lighthouse had been built, but they were allowed to keep their old quarters. The two old people died almost simultaneously; so leaving Marina alone. She belonged to no one, and nobody particularly wished to take charge of her. But, as I have said before she was rather a favourite in the town, when she appeared on market days with her curious wares, for this is how she made her living.

She would gather all manner of curious and iridescent shells and make them into necklaces, or boxes, and such like things. Likewise she made curious bouquets of dried seaweeds. But her chief source of income were the eggs of the gulls, guillemots, sea-swallows, penguins, and the like.

Strange to say, all these wild creatures were perfectly tame to her. They would come to her to be fed, and actually allowed her to take their eggs from their nest. She never took more than one from each nest. She was singularly nimble of foot, and would climb up to their fastnesses.

In this trade she had a speciality. If anyone else had attempted to take their eggs, the assembled water-fowl of all kinds would unanimously and unmercifully have attacked them.

So, once a week, the quaint little figure could be seen crossing in her little boat, which she had painted green herself, encrusted with corals and shells in strange devices.

She was very simply clad in one single loose white garment, bound rather curiously with a sea-green sash made of silk; on one exceptionally lucky day she had found means to purchase this one article of finery, which had always attracted her fancy. She was always barefooted; but she wore shell necklaces and bracelets, and also wore wreaths in her hair of delicate seaweeds.

Her eyes were green; her hair a peculiar nuance, which also in certain lights looked green. So it was not very wonderful for the superstitious people to think her a water-sprite.

So, though living all alone and unprotected, she was quite safe, as no one would dare to rob or molest her. She spent the rest of her time in swimming and rowing about, or running along the rocks in search of various sea-products. Perhaps on these occasions her toilet was less complete than it was on Saturdays.

I am afraid poor Marina was a heathen. Again, what is everybody's business is nobody's business. It was nobody's business to give her religious instruction, or indeed any instruction whatever. The priests in that part are not of a very high order; generally even more superstitious than their flocks. The worthy Padre did not care to come much in contact with the creature he thought not quite human; and besides, there was no one to pay him for instructing her. Indeed some people averred she had never even been baptized.

One day some vague sense of religion did wake in her; she saw in a shop-window an intaglio, in some green stone, representing a venerable-looking old man with a trident, standing between two long tumbled lines of sea, from which emerged beautiful figures of maidens with long streaming hair, and beautiful youths playing on spiral shell-trumpets. This pleased her immensely. So much so that she determined to purchase it at the cost of all her savings, which, I think, amounted to three dollars. So one day she went to the shop, and triumphantly demanded the article, displaying what she supposed to be her vast wealth.

'But, my dear,' said the shopman, 'the price of that is fifty dollars.'

She stood aghast. Fifty dollars! she had never heard of so much money in her life.

Then she began to cry silently.

There happened to be an intellectual-looking Englishman in the shop, who had come to the island in his yacht in search of orchids. He was struck both with the pathos and the humour of the situation. He paid down the fifty dollars, and gave the intaglio to the child.

She could not believe her senses; and disappeared like a flash of lightning, clutching her treasure to her bosom; ran at full speed through the town, jumped into her boat and rowed quickly across, and did not rest till she had reached her airy nest in safety.

She had occasionally wandered into the church, and got a few confused notions of a cult which she did not understand; so, by way of imitation, she hung up the intaglio in the corner of the room, and placed a perpetual light to burn before it.

I may here fitly describe what the room was like. It was hexagonal; she had painted it herself with a curious wavy pattern in her favourite sea-green. But all the corners she had encrusted with shells and seaweed; of which she also had fashioned an elaborate frieze. The furniture was very simple indeed: the only table was utilised to support a large aquarium, which also was a present from a rich foreigner; and that she had arranged with a kind of fairy garden, with seaweeds for trees, and all manner of beautiful sea anemones for flowers. The rest of the furniture consisted of two large boxes: in one box she had made herself a luxurious bed with the shed feathers of the wild sea-birds; in the other box there was something still more extraordinary at the moment this story commences, namely, an albatross sitting upon her egg. There was no chair; for if she sat down at all, she sat on the floor; also no fireplace, as in Varenha it is never cold. And she spent most of her time in the open air; and as she found her food on the sea-shore, she had no need of cooking. Indeed, so self-supporting was she, that she would first make a meal on a mollusc, and then sell the shell.

On exceptional occasions she would treat herself to a seaweed salad, which is by no means so unpalatable as it sounds to those who have never tasted one.

The windows were always open, and the wild sea-birds would fly out and in; she used to buy food for them in the town, which cost her much more than her own food ever did.

But her chief friend was an albatross, whom she called Almotâna, who had made her nest for three successive years in her box. Indeed, when the albatross flew out, Marina would sit on the nest and keep the egg warm herself; which the albatross understood, as she never flew away unless the little girl was there. Once a day during the season another bigger albatross, whom she called Wandafra, would come to visit his wife. But he did not see the fun of sitting on the egg if the little girl would undertake that office for him. How she came to choose these names, which conformed to no known language, is difficult to ascertain. All that is known is that when she was first picked up she gabbled some unintelligible jargon, which ever afterwards she had been heard to murmur to herself.

One day a steamer *did* land at Varenha. It was quasi-private, and more or less going round the world. There were all sorts and conditions of people in it; or rather, I mean, many sorts, but one condition: *e.g.* there were collectors, who wished to land at Varenha to collect various objects which were their particular hobby, and sportsmen who thought it great fun to shoot guillemots; but no steerage passengers.

Among these was a certain German professor, called Sammler. Herr Sammler collected everything. From being a poor professor of zoology and botany, he had unexpectedly come into a considerable fortune. So now he was enabled to indulge his mania to the full.

One Saturday, as usual, Marina went with her wares to the marketplace; it was just at the beginning of the breeding season, and she had an unusually good collection of various eggs.

There came up to her stall a benevolent-looking old gentleman with a long white beard and a pair of spectacles, accompanied by a well-known character in the town, a certain Portuguese Jew, called Levi Mendès, who used to act as guide and interpreter to foreigners who landed at the island. The benevolent-looking gentleman took a great interest in Marina's eggs. His knowledge of Portuguese was somewhat limited; so he had to converse chiefly by means of the interpreter. There seemed to be some dispute between them—in German, a language which of course Marina could not understand. But her quick intelligence divined that the Jew wished to beat down her prices, whereas the German was willing to give her more than she asked. It ended by Herr Sammler—for this was he—giving her more money than she had ever got before. Then Mendès drew Professor Sammler aside, and this was their conversation:—

'You said you particularly wanted to get an albatross egg, Herr Professor. Now that little girl has one. You know they are rather difficult to get.

'I know that,' said the Professor. 'Besides, in this island there is a peculiar variety of albatross. It would be indeed something if I could get one of their eggs.'

'Well,' said the Jew, 'I think I could get it for you—and cheap too. The child does not know the value of money. If you will pardon me saying so, I think it was injudicious of you to give her so much for those other eggs. And of course she has no notion of comparative value.'

'I certainly should not think of taking advantage of a little girl,' said the Professor. 'I will give her a fair price for it. But let us go back, and you can arrange for me to see the egg.'

They came back again to her stall. The Jew said insinuatingly—

'This great Senhor is particularly desirous of seeing your albatross egg. Would you mind showing it to him?'

'Oh no,' said Marina, who was impressed by the benevolent appearance of the stranger, and only too proud of showing off her treasures.

'What time could we most conveniently come?' asked Mendès.

'Oh, to-morrow afternoon at three,' said the little girl. 'Then our Almotâna goes out for her afternoon fly.'

So next day Herr Sammler and his guide presented themselves at the lighthouse, where they found Marina sitting as usual on the egg.

'Isn't it beautiful?' she said, rising and pointing the egg out to the Professor.

'May the Senhor look at it?' asked Levi.

'I don't know whether Almotâna would like it,' said Marina; 'but if he is very careful with it——

The Professor took the egg up in his hand.

Strange is the mania for collecting. People who would otherwise be incapable of dishonest action resort even to theft in order to obtain some rare object which they especially covet.

'Tell her,' said Herr Sammler, 'I will give her twenty dollars for it.'

'The Senhor says he will give you two dollars for it,' says Mendès.

'No, no, no! you must give it me back,' cried Marina.

'No, my dear,' blurted out the German, in very broken Portuguese, 'not two dollars, but twenty dollars—twenty-five dollars!'

'No, this is not to be sold,' cried the little girl. 'Almotâna only lays one egg, and what will she say if she finds her egg gone?'

She began to cry bitterly. But the Professor, under the influence of the lust of collection, calmly put the egg in his pocket, but, being naturally of a kind nature, tried to soothe the child, and produced from his pocket two bank-notes of twenty dollars each.

Marina had never seen a bank-note before. She took the paper, not knowing in the least what it meant.

'You'd better come away,' said Mendès; and hurried Herr Sammler down the stairs.

The child, clutching the bank-notes in her hand, followed them; and her little boat managed to overtake their large boat with four rowers. Then she followed them through the town, saying in piteous monotony—

'Give me back my egg!'

Of course a crowd of people gathered together, and naturally asked what all the fuss was about.

'I do not know what she means,' said Mendès. 'She is mad. See, the Senhor has bought her albatross egg. Here is the egg. And he has given her forty dollars for it. See, she has the forty dollars in her hand.'

And so she had—two crumpled notes, almost crushed to pieces by the sculls of her boat.

The people tried to explain that the Senhor had bought it.

'It is his, and he has given you a very, very great deal of money for it.'

Suddenly Marina attempted to seize the egg from Mendès; and in the scuffle the egg fell to the ground and was smashed.

Marina turned deadly pale, and fell down in a dead faint.

The German, whom I have said before was a kindly man, caused her to be taken to his hotel, and instructed his landlady to put her into the best bed she could find.

The landlady, who was a good kind of woman, and likewise because she wished to oblige the Professor, and feared to do any ill to the water-sprite, treated her with the utmost gentleness.

Marina remained for a long time unconscious, and then reviving to semi-consciousness, fell asleep. Seeing her in a natural sleep the landlady left her. But she did not wake till dawn.

She found herself in a huge room and a large bed. It was some time before she could realise and recollect. Then, clad only in a night-gown as she was, she opened the window, and managed somehow to slide down the water-pipe, and escaped.

When she got to her fastness again, she called out 'Almotâna! Almotâna!' telling as best she could in her strange jargon to the bird what had happened.

There was no answer, but a long wail. She caught sight of the albatross circling round and round, lamenting the loss of her only egg. She went to the window and stretched out her arms and implored Almotâna to come in. But she only continued circling round and wailing.

At last, in her attempts to catch the albatross, she overbalanced herself, and fell straight into the water. Of course the fall was fatal.

A strange thing was to be seen that morning on the seashore: the body of a child in a simple white night-gown washed ashore; standing over it, with wings outspread, an albatross. Just then a boat came in sight—one of the boats from the steamer. In it were two Englishmen. One of them was a thick-set and aggressively muscular young man, of that peculiarly English type; well-formed, perhaps, but wholly without grace; healthy, perhaps, but wholly without bloom, or the expression of vitality, those stupid, dull, apathetic, impudent eyes, peculiar to this breed; features perhaps well-formed, but utterly dull and stolid, without any charm of expression; with a thick, coarse, abundant growth of hair. He was clad in a sort of knickerbocker suit of a loud check pattern, a stick-up collar, and a cap; he carried a gun in his hand.

The other was of a different type: an older man, with something intellectual and refined about his features. 'I say, Jenkins,' said the young man, 'here is a chance: there's an albatross. We shall be able to get one after all. You remember the devil of a fuss we had with that one we hooked: and the bloody brute went and broke the hook, and went off with it.'

'I thought that was horrible!' said the other man. 'The bird was quite tame, and followed the ship for days. Remember the fate of the Ancient Mariner.'

'Damn the Ancient Mariner!' said the other.

'No, I didn't suppose you were familiar with the story of the Ancient Mariner. But there is another consideration of a more practical kind that I wish to urge upon you. You had better not shoot the albatross, because the people here have a kind of superstitious regard for them, and you might get into a great row if you did.'

'What do I care what these damned bloody Portuguese think?' said the young man, taking aim. He shot. And the shot went home.

And at that moment a much larger albatross swooped down, and hit him one terrible blow with his powerful wing. And his companion had little difficulty in ascertaining that he had been killed at once.

Stranger still was the sight that met the eyes of the fisherfolk as they went down to the sea to ply their usual avocation. There was Marina lying dead: and on her bosom the dead albatross, shot through the heart. And circling round, in circles sometimes wide and sometimes narrow, a male albatross, bewailing the death of his mate.

The True Story of a Vampire

VAMPIRE stories are generally located in Styria; mine is also. Styria is by no means the romantic kind of place described by those who have certainly never been there. It is a flat, uninteresting country, only celebrated for its turkeys, its capons, and the stupidity of its inhabitants. Vampires generally arrive at night, in carriages drawn by two black horses.

Our Vampire arrived by the commonplace means of the railway train, and in the afternoon. You must think I am joking, or perhaps that by the word 'Vampire' I mean a financial vampire. No, I am quite serious. The Vampire of whom I am speaking, who laid waste our hearth and home, was a *real* vampire.

Vampires are generally described as dark, sinister-looking, and singularly handsome. Our

Vampire was, on the contrary, rather fair, and certainly was not at first sight sinister-looking, and though decidedly attractive in appearance, not what one would call singularly handsome.

Yes, he desolated our home, killed my brother—the one object of my adoration—also my dear father. Yet, at the same time, I must say that I myself came under the spell of his fascination, and, in spite of all, have no ill-will towards him now.

Doubtless you have read in the papers *passim* of 'the Baroness and her beasts.' It is to tell how I came to spend most of my useless wealth on an asylum for stray animals that I am writing this.

I am old now; what happened then was when I was a little girl of about thirteen. I will begin by describing our household. We were Poles: our name was Wronski: we lived in Styria, where we had a castle. Our household was very limited. It consisted, with the exclusion of domestics, of only my father, our governess—a worthy Belgian named Mademoiselle Vonnaert—my brother, and myself. Let me begin with my father: he was old and both my brother and I were children of his old age. Of my mother I remember nothing: she died in giving birth to my brother, who was only one year, or not as much, younger than myself. Our father was studious, continually occupied in reading books, chiefly on recondite subjects and in all kinds of unknown languages. He had a long white beard, and wore habitually a black velvet skull-cap.

How kind he was to us! It was more than I could tell. Still it was not I who was the favourite. His whole heart went out to Gabriel—Gabryel as we spelt it in Polish. He was always called by the Russian abbreviation Gavril—I mean, of course, my brother, who had a resemblance to the only portrait of my mother, a slight chalk sketch which hung in my father's study. But I was by no means jealous: my brother was and has been the only love of my life. It is for his sake that I am now keeping in Westbourne Park a home for stray cats and dogs.

I was at that time, as I said before, a little girl; my name was Carmela. My long tangled hair was always all over the place, and never would be combed straight. I was not pretty—at least, looking at a photograph of me at that time, I do not think I could describe myself as such. Yet at the same time, when I look at the photograph, I think my expression may have been pleasing to some people: irregular features, large mouth, and large wild eyes.

I was by way of being naughty—not so naughty as Gabriel in the opinion of Mlle. Vonnaert. Mlle. Vonnaert, I may intercalate, was a wholly excellent person, middle-aged, who really *did* speak good French, although she was a Belgian, and could also make herself understood in German, which, as you may or may not know, is the current language of Styria.

I find it difficult to describe my brother Gabriel; there was something about him strange and superhuman, or perhaps I should rather say praeterhuman, something between the animal and the divine. Perhaps the Greek idea of the Faun might illustrate what I mean: but that will not do either. He had large, wild, gazelle-like eyes: his hair, like mine, was in a perpetual tangle—that point he had in common with me, and indeed, as I afterwards heard, our mother having been of gypsy race, it will account for much of the innate wildness there was in our natures. I was wild enough, but Gabriel was much wilder. Nothing would induce him to put on shoes and stockings, except on Sundays—when he also allowed his hair to be combed, but only by me. How shall I describe the grace of that lovely mouth, shaped verily 'en arc d'amour.' I always think of the text in the Psalm, 'Grace is shed forth on thy lips, therefore has God blessed thee eternally'—lips that seemed to exhale the very breath of life. Then that beautiful, lithe, living, elastic form!

He could run faster than any deer: spring like a squirrel to the topmost branch of a tree: he might have stood for the sign and symbol of vitality itself. But seldom could he be induced by Mlle. Vonnaert to learn lessons; but when he did so, he learnt with extraordinary quickness. He would play upon every conceivable instrument, holding a violin here, there, and everywhere except the right place: manufacturing instruments for himself out of reeds—even sticks. Mlle. Vonnaert made futile efforts to induce him to learn to play the piano. I suppose he was what was called spoilt, though merely in the superficial sense of the word. Our father allowed him to indulge in every caprice.

One of his peculiarities, when quite a little child, was horror at the sight of meat. Nothing on earth would induce him to taste it. Another thing which was particularly remarkable about him was his extraordinary power over animals. Everything seemed to come tame to his hand. Birds would sit on his shoulder. Then sometimes Mlle. Vonnaert and I would lose him in the woods—he would suddenly dart away. Then we would find him singing softly or whistling to himself, with all manner of woodland creatures around him—hedgehogs, little foxes, wild rabbits, marmots, squirrels, and such like. He would frequently bring these things home with him and insist on keeping them. This strange menagerie was the terror of poor Mlle. Vonnaert's heart. He chose to live in a little room at the top of a turret; but which, instead of going upstairs, he chose to reach by means of a very tall chestnut-tree, through the window. But in contradiction of all his, it was his custom to serve every Sunday Mass in the parish church, with hair nicely combed and with white surplice and red cassock. He looked as demure and tamed as possible. Then came the element of the divine. What an expression of ecstasy there was in those glorious eyes!

Thus far I have not been speaking about the Vampire. However, let me begin with my narrative at last. One day my father had to go to the neighbouring town—as he frequently had. This time he returned accompanied by a guest. The gentleman, he said, had missed his train, through the late arrival of another at our station, which was a junction, and he would therefore, as trains were not frequent in our parts, have had to wait there all night. He had joined in conversation with my father in the too-late-arriving train from the town: and had consequently accepted my father's invitation to stay the night at our house. But of course, you know, in those out-of-the-way parts we are almost patriarchal in our hospitality.

He was announced under the name of Count Vardalek—the name being Hungarian. But he spoke German well enough: not with the monotonous accentuation of Hungarians, but rather, if anything, with a slight Slavonic intonation. His voice was peculiarly soft and insinuating. We soon afterwards found that he could talk Polish, and Mlle. Vonnaert vouched for his good French. Indeed he seemed to know all languages. But let me give my first impressions. He was rather tall with fair wavy hair, rather long, which accentuated a certain effeminacy about his smooth face. His figure had something—I cannot say what— serpentine about it. The features were refined; and he had long, slender, subtle, magnetic-looking hands, a somewhat long sinuous nose, a graceful mouth, and an attractive smile, which belied the intense sadness of the expression of the eyes. When he arrived his eyes were half closed—indeed they were habitually so—so that I could not decide their colour. He looked worn and wearied. I could not possibly guess his age.

Suddenly Gabriel burst into the room: a yellow butterfly was clinging to his hair. He was carrying in his arms a little squirrel. Of course he was barelegged as usual. The stranger looked up at his approach; then I noticed his eyes. They were green: they seemed to dilate and grow larger. Gabriel stood stock-still, with a startled look, like that of a bird fascinated by a serpent. But nevertheless he held out his hand to the newcomer. Vardalek, taking his hand—I don't know why I noticed this trivial thing—pressed the pulse with his forefinger. Suddenly Gabriel darted from the room and rushed upstairs, going to his turret-room this time by the staircase instead of the tree. I was in terror what the Count might think of him. Great was my relief when he came down in his velvet Sunday suit, and shoes and stockings. I combed his hair, and set him generally right.

When the stranger came down to dinner his appearance had somewhat altered; he looked much younger. There was an elasticity of the skin, combined with a delicate complexion, rarely to be found in a man. Before, he had struck me as being very pale.

Well, at dinner we were all charmed with him, especially my father. He seemed to be thoroughly acquainted with all my father's particular hobbies.

Once, when my father was relating some of his military experiences, he said something about a drummer-boy who was wounded in battle. His eyes opened completely again and dilated: this time with a particularly disagreeable expression, dull and dead, yet at the same time animated by some horrible excitement. But this was only momentary.

The chief subject of his conversation with my father was about certain curious mystical books which my father had just lately picked up, and which he could not make out, but Vardalek seemed completely to understand. At dessert-time my father asked him if he were in a great hurry to reach his destination: if not, would he not stay with us a little while: though our place was out of the way, he would find much that would interest him in his library.

He answered, 'I am in no hurry. I have no particular reason for going to that place at all, and if I can be of service to you in deciphering these books, I shall be only too glad.' He added with a smile which was bitter, very very bitter: 'You see I am a cosmopolitan, a wanderer on the face of the earth.'

After dinner my father asked him if he played the piano. He said, 'Yes, I can a little,' and he sat down at the piano. Then he played a Hungarian csardas—wild, rhapsodic, wonderful.

That is the music which makes men mad. He went on in the same strain. Gabriel stood stock-still by the piano, his eyes dilated and fixed, his form quivering. At last he said very slowly, at one particular motive—for want of a better word you may call it the *relâche* of a csardas, by which I mean that point where the original quasi-slow movement begins again—'Yes, I think I could play that.'

Then he quickly fetched his fiddle and self-made xylophone, and did, actually alternating the instruments, render the same very well indeed. Vardalek looked at him, and said in a very sad voice, 'Poor child! you have the soul of music within you.' I could not understand why he should seem to commiserate instead of congratulate Gabriel on what certainly showed an extraordinary talent.

Gabriel was shy even as the wild animals who were tame to him. Never before had he taken to a stranger. Indeed, as a rule, if any stranger came to the house by any chance, he would hide himself, and I had to bring him up his food to the turret chamber. You may imagine what was my surprise when I saw him walking about hand in hand with Vardalek the next morning, in the garden, talking lively with him, and showing his collection of pet animals, which he had gathered from the woods, and for which we had had to fit up a regular zoological gardens. He seemed utterly under the domination of Vardalek. What surprised us was (for otherwise we liked the stranger, especially for being kind to him) that he seemed, though not noticeably at first—except perhaps to me, who noticed everything with regard to him—to be gradually losing his general health and vitality. He did not become pale as yet; but there was a certain languor about his movements which certainly there was by no means before.

My father got more and more devoted to Count Vardalek. He helped him in his studies: and my father would hardly allow him to go away, which he did sometimes—to Trieste, he said: he always came back, bringing us presents of strange Oriental jewellery or textures.

I knew all kinds of people came to Trieste, Orientals included. Still, there was a strangeness and magnificence about these things which I was sure even then could not possibly have come from such a place as Trieste, memorable to me chiefly for its necktie shops.

When Vardalek was away, Gabriel was continually asking for him and talking about him. Then at the same time he seemed to regain his old vitality and spirits. Vardalek always returned looking much older, wan, and weary. Gabriel would rush to meet him, and kiss him on the mouth. Then he gave a slight shiver: and after a little while began to look quite young again.

Things continued like this for some time. My father would not hear of Vardalek's going away permanently. He came to be an inmate of our house. I indeed, and Mlle. Vonnaert also, could not help noticing what a difference there was altogether about Gabriel. But my father seemed totally blind to it.

One night I had gone downstairs to fetch something which I had left in the drawing-room. As I was going up again I passed Vardalek's room. He was playing on a piano, which had been specially put there for him, one of Chopin's nocturnes, very beautifully: I stopped, leaning on the banisters to listen.

Something white appeared on the dark staircase. We believed in ghosts in our part. I was transfixed with terror, and clung to the ballisters.

What was my astonishment to see Gabriel walking slowly down the staircase, his eyes fixed as though in a trance! This terrified me even more than a ghost would. Could I believe my senses? Could that be Gabriel?

I simply could not move. Gabriel, clad in his long white night-shirt, came downstairs and opened the door. He left it open. Vardalek still continued playing, but talked as he played.

He said—this time speaking in Polish—*Nie umiem wyrazic jak ciehie kocham,*—'My darling, I fain would spare thee: but thy life is my life, and I must live, I who would rather die. Will God not have *any* mercy on me? Oh! Oh! life; oh, the torture of life!' Here he struck one agonized and strange chord, then continued playing softly, 'O, Gabriel, my beloved! my life, yes *life*—oh, why life? I am sure this is but a little that I demand of thee. Surely thy superabundance of life can spare a little to one who is already dead. No, stay,' he said now almost harshly, 'what must be, must be!'

Gabriel stood there quite still, with the same fixed vacant expression, in the room. He was evidently walking in his sleep. Vardalek played on: then said, 'Ah!' with a sign of terrible agony. Then very gently, 'Go now, Gabriel; it is enough.' And Gabriel went out of the room and ascended the staircase at the same slow pace, with the same unconscious stare. Vardalek struck the piano, and although he did not play loudly, it seemed as though the strings would break. You never heard music so strange and so heart-rending!

I only know I was found by Mlle. Vonnaert in the morning, in an unconscious state, at the foot of the stairs. Was it a dream after all? I am sure now that it was not. I thought then it might be, and said nothing to anyone about it. Indeed, what could I say?

Well, to let me cut a long story short, Gabriel, who had never known a moment's sickness in his life, grew ill: and we had to send to Gratz for a doctor, who could give no explanation of Gabriel's strange illness. Gradual wasting away, he said: absolutely no organic complaint. What could this mean?

My father at last became conscious of the fact that Gabriel was ill. His anxiety was fearful. The last trace of grey faded from his hair, and it became quite white. We sent to Vienna for doctors. But all with the same result.

Gabriel was generally unconscious, and when conscious, only seemed to recognize Vardalek, who sat continually by his bedside, nursing him with the utmost tenderness.

One day I was alone in the room: and Vardalek cried suddenly, almost fiercely, 'Send for a priest at once, at once,' he repeated. 'It is now almost too late!'

Gabriel stretched out his arms spasmodically, and put them round Vardalek's neck. This was the only movement he had made, for some time. Vardalek bent down and kissed him on the lips. I rushed downstairs: and the priest was sent for. When I came back Vardalek was not there. The priest administered extreme unction. I think Gabriel was already dead, although we did not think so at the time.

Vardalek had utterly disappeared; and when we looked for him he was nowhere to be found; nor have I seen or heard of him since.

My father died very soon afterwards: suddenly aged, and bent down with grief. And so the whole of the Wronski property came into my sole possession. And here I am, an old woman, generally laughed at for keeping, in memory of Gabriel, an asylum for stray animals—and—people do not, as a rule, believe in Vampires!

The Worm of Luck

'NO, mamma does not love me any longer; and as to papa, I hate him.'

Thus spoke a boy of fourteen, with proud, defiant dark eyes, standing in the middle of a wood. He was hatless, with wind-blown hair, but nevertheless smartly clad. In appearance he was very like the well-known John the Baptist of Andrea del Sarto. He was thinking of many things, indeed of his whole life. His own father he could remember but dimly. He only remembered, when he was quite a little child, a dark man, who was very kind to him, and who, every night, sent him to sleep by a peculiar lullaby, played on a fiddle. Then he remembered a life of tents and caravans and wanderings; then he was suddenly transferred to a luxurious villa on the Adriatic. At first all went fairly well. His step-father was amiable to him, and gave him toys, and his mother rigged him out in elegant sailor suits with gold braid, and he became the pet of all the ladies in the neighbourhood. He heard one time his step-father remark, 'Really, I don't despair of turning Sandor into a gentleman.' He did not quite understand what it meant, but somehow, the remark galled him. Then there came a hitch. A baby was born. Then the Graf von Gratheim, having a son and heir, took an aversion to the child of the beautiful gypsy woman, whom he had married in a moment of excessive passion, as the daughters of the gypsies do not give themselves otherwise.

Sandor was passionately fond of music, and, like every gypsy child, could play the fiddle very well. His step-father detested music. Then again, he himself had a particular aversion to the baby which he erroneously thought supplanted himself in his mother's affection. He would not even be in the same room where the baby was. So things got from bad to worse, and that day, when the baby was about three years old, he was sitting in a nook in the drawing-room, improvising on his fiddle, quite concealed by palm-trees and oleanders—so concealed and inspired, that he did not notice his step-father coming in.

His step-father said furiously, 'Ah! that's you, *Gypsy*! Shut up your infernal row! You're really not fit for civilised society. I heartily wish you would go back to your own people.' His eyes flashed fire, and he went out of the room without a word, and out of the house into the woods, taking nothing with him but his fiddle.

Suddenly he heard through the trees a sound of stringed instruments—a xylophone playing gypsy music. He looked out stealthily, and saw three men. Then they ceased playing. The first man said, 'Where shall we go to-day; to the right or the left?' The second said, 'Perhaps we had better go to the right for there there's a town.' The third man said, 'No, we must be returning home; you know next Sunday is the Day of Shadows, and we have hardly time to get back.' The first man answered, 'Oh, of course. I had forgotten that. We must be getting off at once.'

Suddenly the boy darted out from the trees and cried, 'Oh, take me with you. I can play the fiddle a little too.'

The first man said, very kindly and tenderly, 'Yes, little one, we'll take you with us, but remember ours is a hard life. We gypsies don't sleep on feather-beds.'

The second man said, 'Why, I believe he belongs to our race.'

The third man took his sleeve and bared his arm. 'Why,' he cried, 'that is the mark of our clan. What does it all mean?'

The boy fainted with exhaustion and excitement. The first man took him in his arms and carried him along. Then he said, 'How like he is to Sandor!' The boy revived for a moment, and murmured, 'Yes, my name is Sandor. I was called after my father,' and then fainted again. The second man said, 'Oh, yes, I understand it all. He must be the son of Gisela, who disgraced our race by marrying an alien.' The third man said, 'You see gypsy blood will never be tamed. He has come back to his own people.'

'Yes,' said the boy, suddenly vitalised, 'I will go back to my own people. He called me "gypsy" to-day!'

'My dear,' said the first man, 'do you know that you are my brother's son? I am your uncle Ferencz.'

'Oh, yes,' said the boy, 'I thought I had seen you before.'

So Sandor went with the men, and arrived at their more or less permanent quarters, and soon accommodated himself to their life. He was told that if he discovered an owl's nest during that week, and could take one egg from it to bury it under a hazel-tree, after exactly seven years he would find the worm of luck in the same place. Owls' nests are not easy to find, but for anyone who wishes to find their eggs they have one advantage, that the owl lays a second batch of eggs whilst the former are still in the nest, so by good luck it is possible to secure one whilst she is leaving her nest to procure food for her children. One night he saw some small animal running on the ground, then a great white owl, with a shrill hissing cry, leapt from her nest and seized upon it. Meanwhile, quick as thought, Sandor sprang up the tree, and found one egg still unhatched, and buried it duly under a hazel-tree.

On the 23rd of April he was selected by the clan to represent 'Green George.' He was stripped and garlanded with leaves, then he was pursued about the place like Dionysus. He was a little frightened at this; he thought he was going to be sacrificed, but he said to himself, 'Better be sacrificed for my own people than live there with *them.*' But he was not sacrificed, only thrown in to the water in effigy.

For seven years he dwelt with his clan. On the day he had buried the owl's egg, on digging, he found a long green caterpillar, which he ate.

He had always played the fiddle remarkably well, but every one was astonished at the manner he played that night. The gypsies themselves were dumfounded by his originality and inspiration.

So the long and short of it was that Sandor should go and wander alone and play the fiddle, and get money for the clan. In one small town he came to, an old Professor came up to him and said, 'Why, you play wonderfully. I never heard anyone play like you. What is so specially wonderful is that you manage to evoke so much out of an old cracked fiddle like that. Come with me, and I will give you a Stradivarius violin, which has come into my hands as a legacy, and which I cannot play myself. All I ask in recompense is that you should play to me once upon it.' Sandor accepted. Then for the first time he realised himself his own power. In the next town he came to he boldly advertised a concert. The entertainment was given entirely by himself. It was a small but rather fashionable place during its season. The fashionable people, having little distraction, all came out of curiosity to hear 'der Grüner Georg,' who advertised himself for a concert. (He always called himself now by the name of 'Grüner Georg,' especially as he was now nearing places where he had been before.) The audience was spellbound, and from that time he created a *furore*. Money (the greater part of which he remitted to his clan) poured into his hands; he also became a lion of society. Fortunately for him, though a gypsy, he had at one time of his life been familiar with the ways of society—but all this did not turn his head. He sighed for the old wild life again.

One day in his wanderings he came back to the place where he used to live.

'Ha, ha!' he said, 'they don't know that "Grüner Georg" means me!'

Tired of luxuries, he often would go out into the woods, and sleep in the open air. This time he determined he would go and sleep exactly there whence he had run away seven years before. He sat there playing to himself on his violin, thinking again of all his past life, when a boy came out from the trees and said, 'Oh, I love music. Will you let me listen to you?'

'Certainly,' he said. 'What would you like me to play to you?'

'Oh, anything you like,' said the boy, seating himself at his feet. 'Father hates music, and won't allow any music in the house; but I love music, especially this sort of music.'

He played on and on; then he said to the child, 'Tell me, what is your name?'

'Mother calls me Gyula,' he answered, 'but father calls me Julius or Jules, because he says he can't bear Hungarian names.'

'Then who is your mother?' he asked.

'Oh! my mother is Countess von Gratheim.'

'The Countess von Gratheim was my mother too,' said Sandor.

'Then' said the child, looking puzzled, 'you must be my brother.'

'Yes, dear,' said he, kissing him. 'You are indeed my brother.'

'Then,' said he, 'what is your name? '

'I have no surname,' he answered, 'but my Christian name is Sandor.'

'Sandor?' said the child, 'Why, only yesterday mother was saying, "Oh! if I only knew what has become of poor Sandor!" and father said, "Don't mention his name. He is very well named Sandor, as he has brought 'schande'[1] on our family." I don't know in the least what he meant,' added the child innocently.

'However,' said Sandor, somewhat bitterly, 'it is not *poor* Sandor now. I have plenty of money. I

---

1 Sandor is pronounced *Sh*andor, Gyula, *D*yula.

dare say you may have heard of me. I go generally by the name of Grüner Georg.'

'Why,' said the boy, '*you* Grüner Georg! I have been saving up all my pocket-money to hear you, and I was going to slip out on the sly one day and go to one of your concerts. Papa wouldn't let me otherwise, because, I don't know why, he can't bear anything to do with gypsies, and now I have heard you for nothing.'

'My dear child,' said the young man, 'you also have something to do with gypsies. Mother is a gypsy, as perhaps you don't know.'

It was late autumn, and singularly mild; but while they were talking the sun had set, and it was quite dark.

'Child,' said Sandor, 'you cannot possibly go home now, but if you will stay here, I promise to take you home to-morrow morning. I know the way,' he added, with a trace of bitterness. 'Look here, I will wrap you in my fur coat. I can make you a very nice bed and pillow out of dead leaves. I am quite clever at that. It is not very cold after all.' Then he murmured to himself between his teeth. '*He* shall see that gypsy blood can never be tamed.'

'But,' said the child, 'you will be cold yourself.'

'Oh dear no!' said Sandor. 'I am quite used to lie on the bare ground. We *gypsies*' (he said this in the same contemptuous tone that, seven years ago, he step-father had used to him) 'do not lie upon feather-beds.'

So he wrapped the child in his mantle, and made him a comfortable bed of leaves. The child, who was growing sleepy, said, 'Sandor, my brother, won't you play me one thing more?'

'Yes, dear, I will,' he said. Then he played the lullaby with which his own father used to send him to sleep. It had the same effect upon Gyula; then he himself ultimately lay down by the side of his little brother. A wind arose, a number of leaves were blown upon Grüner Georg, making a complete coverlet.

'I was once Green George,' he said, somewhat sadly, 'now, I suppose, I am Yellow George,' and he fell asleep too.

There was, as there often is in those parts, a quite sudden change of temperature during the night. Thick flakes of snow began to fall, the first of the year, and enveloped the two as in a shroud. Then a sudden hard frost set in. Neither noticed; both were fast asleep, Gyula leaning his head upon his brother's shoulder. But the sudden frost killed both the delicately nurtured child and the strong young man.

*

If anyone had been there they would certainly have been much surprised to see on that unprecedentedly cold morning a very elegantly dressed lady wandering distractedly through the woods, crying almost wildly, 'Gyula! Gyula!' making distracted appeals, 'O God! have I not lost one, that I should lose the other too!'

She came upon the place where they were lying, almost armoured with a frozen sheet of snow.

'Gyula!' she cried. 'What are you doing here?' Then she looked and recognised. 'Sandor, my own, my firstborn! you here! 'She flung herself upon him and kissed him passionately. 'I am your mother, don't you know me? Wake up! Speak to me!' Neither of them moved. Then she gradually realised. She did not weep at all. She took off her cloak of rich sable, and laid it as a pall over the bodies of her two children. Then she took off all her rings and jewellery, and, cutting off a long tress of her black hair, threaded them together with it, then yoked her two sons together with this strange necklace.

'I will go back to my own people,' she said, and went forth into the woods.

A PARTIAL LIST OF SNUGGLY BOOKS

CPSIA information can be obtained
at www.ICGtesting.com
Printed in the USA
BVHW071438201221
624504BV00007B/945